JAN KARON

The Trellis and the Seed

A BOOK OF ENCOURAGEMENT

⇥ FOR ALL AGES ⇤

Paintings by Robert Gantt Steele

VIKING

VIKING
Published by Penguin Group
Penguin Young Readers Group, 345 Hudson Street, New York, New York 10014, U.S.A.
Penguin Books Ltd, 80 Strand, London WC2R 0RL, England
Penguin Books Australia Ltd, 250 Camberwell Road, Camberwell, Victoria 3124, Australia
Penguin Books Canada Ltd, 10 Alcorn Avenue, Toronto, Ontario, Canada M4V 3B2
Penguin Books (N.Z.) Ltd, 182-190 Wairau Road, Auckland 10, New Zealand

First published in 2003 by Viking, a division of Penguin Young Readers Group.

3 5 7 9 10 8 6 4 2

Text copyright © Jan Karon, 2003
Illustrations copyright © Robert Gantt Steele, 2003

LIBRARY OF CONGRESS CATALOGING-IN-PUBLICATION DATA
Karon, Jan, date-
The trellis and the seed / by Jan Karon ; illustrated Robert Gantt Steele.
p. cm.
Summary: A small seed surprises itself by becoming a flowering moonflower vine.
ISBN 0-670-89289-0 (hardcover)
[1. Seeds—Fiction. 2. Moonflower—Fiction. 3. Flowers—Fiction. 4.Growth—Fiction.]
I. Steele, Robert Gantt, ill. II. Title.
PZ7.K146 Tr 2003   [E]—dc21   2002015752

Printed in U.S.A.
Set in Mrs. Eaves

"Every good gift and every perfect gift is from above . . ." *James 1:17*

In memory of Rosie Potter;
tender spirit,
devoted companion,
good and perfect gift.
—J.K.

To my beloved wife Alice,
who always has hidden strength
and radiant beauty.
—R.G.S.

The little seed felt warm in the Nice Lady's hand.

Someone had given it to her at the end of summer, because she had a garden and loved flowers.

"Here," they said, "this will make a beautiful vine with sweet-smelling blossoms."

The little seed, however, did not believe this. It was only a seed, and very, very small. How could it ever be a beautiful vine with blossoms?

The little seed spent the winter
in a jelly glass on the top shelf of a
china cupboard.

When spring came, the Nice Lady went out and bought a trellis for the seed.

A whole trellis for one tiny seed!

Then she took down the glass and ran a bit of water into it, so the seed could soak.

"This will make you soft and help you sprout faster," she said.

The Nice Lady went to her early spring garden and found just the right place for the trellis.

She put it deep into the ground by her brick wall. At the base, she made a tiny hole with her finger. Then she went inside and picked up the seed, which had grown soft from soaking.

She took it to the garden.

She put it in the hole.

She said, "Good-bye! See you this summer!"

Then she filled the small hole with dirt and patted it firmly with her hand.

Though being someplace soft felt
nice for a change, it was *dark* in the
hole. It was *cold* in the hole.

Don't worry, said the Earth. *God has
planned something beautiful for you. You will
be a green vine with blossoms that scent the air
with sweet perfume.*

There it was again. That story about
vines and blossoms! The little seed did
not believe it.

Days passed. The sun shone and the rain fell.

And then there was a stir in the small, dark hole.

First something happened at the bottom of the little seed.

It felt like a tickle.

Then, something happened at the top of the little seed.

It felt like a kiss.

The rain fell. The sun shone. The days grew warm.

Soon there was no more seed. Instead, there was a small green sprout.

"Hello!" said the Nice Lady. "I knew you'd soon be up and about! Now, if you'll just climb this trellis, I shall be pleased as anything!"

Climb the trellis? How could a small sprout climb a trellis that was a million trillion feet high?

Just start, said the Earth. *The job is half done when you've made a beginning.*

For many days, thunder shook the
heavens. Water stood in puddles in
the garden. The little sprout thought
it might drown.

And then the sun came out. It shone and shone.

While the sprout was scarcely paying attention, it became a vine.

The vine stretched out a green, curling tendril. It touched something that didn't feel soft like dirt or warm like sun.

For a moment, it was afraid of anything that felt so different, and tried to pull its tendril back. But it was stuck to the trellis.

There was only one thing to do. It began to climb.

It couldn't help climbing! It couldn't stop climbing!

It climbed to the right and climbed to the left.

It danced out into the air where there was no trellis at all.

Then one day, it couldn't climb any higher.

It tried and tried to reach the top of the trellis, but nothing worked.

Its glossy leaves drooped. Its tendrils lost their lively curl.

The Nice Lady came out and, humming a little tune, sprinkled something smelly around the roots of the vine. Then she worked it into the earth with her spade. "There!" she said to the vine. "That should be *delicious!*"

Soon afterward, a summer shower swept over the garden. And suddenly, the top of the trellis didn't seem so far away, after all.

Foxgloves and hollyhocks blossomed by the doorstep.

Cosmos and lavender bordered the path.

Old-fashioned roses twined up an arbor, spilling petals onto ruffled petunias.

In the Nice Lady's garden, everything was blooming. Everything but the vine on the trellis.

Though it had climbed all the way to the top of the trellis and started up the brick wall, it felt very disappointed. For it knew, at last, that the story about fragrant blossoms wasn't true at all.

Wait, said the Earth. *God's timing for you is different.*

That evening, a full moon appeared in the cloudless sky. It rose slowly over the Nice Lady's house, turning the garden path into a ribbon of silver.

The vine felt the soft moonlight steal among its leaves.

Something happened that felt like a tickle.

Then something happened that felt like a kiss.

Soon the Nice Lady appeared in her nightdress and bare feet, walking on the silver ribbon.

"What's going on?" she asked the garden. "A wondrous fragrance awakened me and called me to come out!"

She followed the scent until she came to the trellis. There, half hidden among the leaves, she saw dozens of ivory blossoms unfolding on the vine. As each blossom opened, a heavenly aroma escaped upon the air, bathing the garden with sweet perfume.

The Nice Lady looked on in amazement. She could hardly believe that so much beauty and mystery had come from one tiny seed.

"I just knew you were going to be something wonderfully different!" she exclaimed.

Happily she twined an ivory blossom in her hair.

She tucked another in a buttonhole of her nightdress.

She picked an especially beautiful bloom to put by her bed in a painted china cup.

"Thank you!" she said, filled with admiration.

As she walked back to her house on the silver ribbon, a shiver of joy stirred in the vine that blooms only at night— the vine whose lovely name is Moonflower.

And over the Nice Lady's garden,

there was stillness and peace.